MAGIC IN THE MARGINS

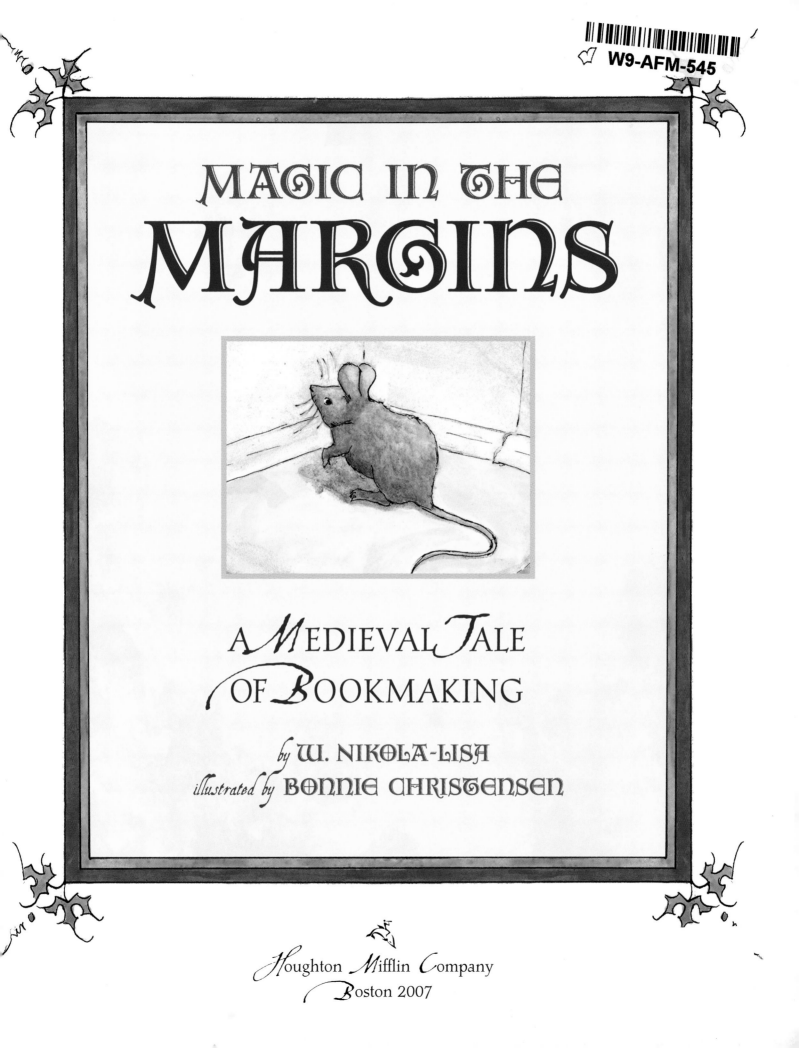

A MEDIEVAL TALE OF BOOKMAKING

by W. NIKOLA-LISA

illustrated by BONNIE CHRISTENSEN

Houghton Mifflin Company
Boston 2007

To Herb and Jean, for a life well traveled. —W. N.-L.

For Gianfranco. —B.C.

Text copyright © 2007 by W. Nikola-Lisa
Illustrations copyright © 2007 by Bonnie Christensen

www.houghtonmifflinbooks.com

The text of this book is set in Post Mediaeval.
The illustrations are ink and egg tempera.

Library of Congress Cataloging-in-Publication Data

Nikola-Lisa, W.
Magic in the margins : a medieval tale of bookmaking /
by W. Nikola-Lisa ; illustrations by Bonnie Christensen.
p. cm.
Summary: At a medieval monastery, orphaned Simon, who is apprenticing in illumination,
dreams of the day he can create his own pictures, but finds he must first complete a
strange and unusual assignment that Father Anselm has given him.
ISBN-13: 978-0-618-49642-6 (hardcover)
ISBN-10: 0-618-49642-4 (hardcover)
[1. Artists—Fiction. 2. Illumination of books and manuscripts—Fiction. 3. Apprentices—Fiction.
4. Orphans—Fiction.] I. Christensen, Bonnie, ill. II. Title.
PZ7.N5855Ma 2007   [Fic]—dc22
2006017060

Printed in Singapore
TWA 10 9 8 7 6 5 4 3 2 1

PREFACE

The inspiration for this story came, as often happens, from another book. In this case it was Elizabeth B. Wilson's *Bibles and Bestiaries: A Guide to Illuminated Manuscripts* (1994), produced in collaboration with the Pierpont Morgan Library in New York. In the book, Ms. Wilson includes an illustration from an edition of St. Augustine's *City of God*, written around A.D. 1140.

The illustration is of a scribe, Hildebertus, who spies a "pesky mouse" stealing his cheese. Pictured below the irritated Hildebertus is his young apprentice, who continues to paint border designs on a scrap of parchment, oblivious to Hildebertus's annoyance.

Although Hildebertus and the mouse dominate the scene, I couldn't help but wonder about the young apprentice. How did he come to work in a monastery's scriptorium? What was his education or training like? Would he ever become an accomplished artist himself?

Like so many stories, this one welled up from the questions I posed.

I t was not unusual in Europe during the Middle Ages for a nobleman's son to be taken in by the Church. Many sons of wealthy men made the Church their home.

Simon was different, however. He was not a nobleman's son. He was an orphan, the son of peasants who perished in the spring floods.

But Simon's quick grasp of things and his keen wit made it hard for the brothers of the monastery at which he appeared to turn him away.

The task of educating Simon fell to Brother William, a monk and master scribe who worked in the monastery's scriptorium, or writing room. It was under Brother William's guidance that Simon learned the ways of the scriptorium: how to make parchment, a writing surface made from sheepskin; how to cure quill pens; how to grind pigments to make paint; and how to form the letters of the alphabet.

It was also under Brother William's tutelage that Simon learned about the different man-uscripts, or handmade books, in the monastery's scriptorium.

He learned that a Bestiary was a book about animals, both real and imagined.

He learned that an Herbal described plants used for medicines and that a Psalter was a collection of psalms from the Bible.

Simon was an eager student and he couldn't wait to help Father Anselm, the monastery's abbot and master illuminator, draw the pic-tures for one of the monastery's manuscripts.

First, though, Brother William wanted Simon to practice, and so the young apprentice spent hours sketching on scraps of parchment. A leaf pattern here. A twisting vine pattern there.

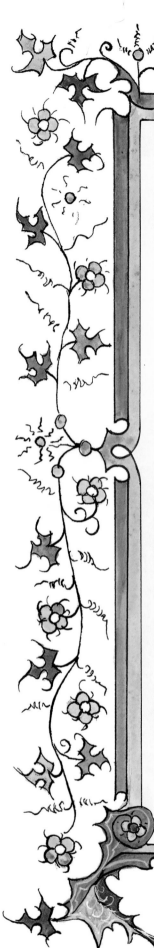

One day, after he had completed another set of exercises, Simon asked, "When will I get to draw pictures of my own in one of Father Anselm's manuscripts?"

"Patience, Simon," Brother William responded. "It was years before I was allowed to try my hand on anything but a scrap of parchment. You have progressed quicker than any apprentice I have ever had."

"But I am ready to do more than draw leaf patterns on scraps of parchment—"

"Simon, you are very talented," Brother William interrupted. "I have no doubt that your drawings will adorn the pages of many illuminated manuscripts one day, but that is something only Father Anselm can decide."

Simon's gaze fell to the ground.

"Of course, if you'd like," Brother William added, "I will take the matter up with Father Anselm."

Simon's eyes brightened.

Father Anselm was a tall, gaunt man with chiseled features, stern in his demeanor, but clever and wise.

When Brother William told Simon several days later that he had spoken to Father Anselm and that the abbot would see him, Simon trembled with excitement.

When they arrived at Father Anselm's chamber, the abbot was seated at his desk, studying several large scraps of parchment.

"Ah, Simon," Father Anselm said, looking up, "I've been waiting for you. Brother William has given me samples of your drawings."

To Simon's surprise, the parchment scraps contained some of the studies he had recently completed.

"Brother William tells me you are an excellent apprentice," Father Anselm continued.

Simon nodded timidly.

"And that you desire to draw pictures in one of my manuscripts."

Simon nodded again.

ell, your drawings are quite good," continued Father Anselm. "You have a good eye, and it appears that you can copy anything. But talent is not enough, Simon. To be an artist you must have both skill and vision."

"Vision?" Simon asked.

"Yes, the greatest artists are not those who merely copy pictures. The greatest artists create new, wonderful images from their imagination."

Simon nodded, pretending to understand.

"To put your hand to a manuscript, you must first demonstrate this ability."

"How shall I do that?" Simon asked nervously.

"By capturing mice, Simon, that's how!" exclaimed Father Anselm.

"Capturing mice?"

"Yes. The monastery has been plagued with them lately. I want you to capture as many as you can. But a word of caution," Father Anselm added. "Mice are tricky little creatures. You must study them, get to know them inside and out—and remember, *use your imagination!*"

For the next few weeks, Simon tried as hard as he could to catch mice. He chased them. Dove at them. Threw scraps of parchment at them. Set traps for them. It was a more difficult task than he had thought.

One day, as he sat copying leaf patterns on a scrap of parchment in the scriptorium, Simon noticed a mouse crouched several feet away. Setting the parchment aside, Simon flung himself at the tiny creature. But the beady-eyed mouse scampered away, leaving Simon face down on the floor—just as the door opened.

ather Anselm!" Simon exclaimed, looking up.

"Simon?" Father Anselm replied in surprise.

"I was trying to catch a mouse," Simon stammered, "as you instructed, Good Father."

ut I didn't ask you to catch mice," Father Anselm said after a moment of silence. "I asked you to capture them. There's quite a difference between the two."

Having thus spoken, Father Anselm walked down the hallway, leaving Simon to ponder his words.

hat does he mean," Simon asked Brother William when he arrived at the scriptorium later, " 'I didn't ask you to catch mice . . . I asked you to capture them'? Isn't that the same thing?"

Brother William thought for a moment. "It appears Father Anselm has posed a puzzle for you. My advice is to follow Father Anselm's words exactly. Do you remember what he told you in his chamber?"

"Yes," replied Simon. "That in order to capture mice, I must study them, know them inside and out, and that I must use my imagination!"

"Yes, I see," mused Brother William, scratching his head in bewilderment. "A puzzle, indeed."

That night, as Simon lay on his pallet in the dormitory, he could think of nothing else but Father Anselm's mysterious words. He turned them over and over in his mind until he noticed something quivering in the corner—*a mouse!*

As he turned his gaze to it, Father Anselm's words flashed into his mind: *You must study them, know them inside and out.*

Simon fixed his eyes on the tiny creature, noting its every detail. What surprised him was how alert and watchful the mouse seemed. How it twitched at the slightest noise. And how quickly it turned and disappeared.

Simon kept these thoughts in his mind as he slipped out of the dormitory and into the scriptorium. Drenched in the moon's silver light, Simon filled a small roll of parchment with as many sketches of the mouse as he could possibly render. When he had finished, Simon crept back to the dormitory and fell asleep.

The next morning, Simon found Brother William in the courtyard. "Brother William," he shouted, "I understand! I understand!"

"Understand what?" Brother William asked.

"I understand Father Anselm's puzzle," Simon said.

"And what is that?"

"He wants to see how well I can draw mice, not catch them. That's what he means by capturing them."

I've got to show Father Anselm!" Simon exclaimed, and before Brother William could say a word, Simon turned and scampered away.

Simon headed straight for Father Anselm's chamber. But as he rounded the corner of the chapel, Simon ran headlong into Father Anselm.

H old, my boy," the senior monk scolded. "The monastery is no place for running."

"I'm sorry, Good Father," Simon said. "But I was hurrying to see you. I understand your puzzle."

"Oh, I see," said Father Anselm. "And what is it that you understand?"

Simon pulled the roll of parchment from his belt and showed Father Anselm his drawings.

Father Anselm studied them for a long time. "These are excellent drawings, Simon," he said at last. "You have certainly understood what I meant by studying your subject, getting to know it inside and out, but you have not understood the puzzle completely."

"I haven't?" Simon said, disappointed.

"There are two parts to the puzzle. The first one you have understood, but the second part—'to use your imagination'— you have yet to grasp." Father Anselm handed Simon his drawings and walked away, leaving the boy to think.

After evening prayers, instead of going to the dormitory, Simon stole into the scriptorium to further contemplate Father Anselm's words. Standing inside the doorway, Simon studied the contents of the chamber: Brother William's writing table, a row of ink pots, several cabinets lining the far wall.

The cabinets housed the monastery's manuscripts. Simon had passed them many times during the day, but now, at night, they seemed to beckon him. Although he should have sought Father Anselm's permission, Simon soon found himself sprawled on the floor, paging through one of the large works.

Simon studied the evenly flowing script. He examined the smartly colored paintings. He marveled at the intricately designed headings.

But what most caught Simon's eye were the margins. Here were the most ingenious drawings he had ever seen.

Simon thought of what Brother William had once told him: "The task of making a manuscript is often painfully slow. Each word is copied one letter at a time. Each picture is planned well before it is painted. The work is annoyingly tedious, but it is never without humor."

With this in mind, Simon looked closer at the fanciful drawings in the margins.

What humor! What playfulness! *What imagination!*

Simon stopped. Is this what Father Anselm meant when he said that the greatest artists are not those who merely copy pictures, but those who create new, wonderful images from their imagination?

As Simon thought about this, something else caught his eye— a small, whisker-twitching mouse that crouched at the base of Father Anselm's desk.

Simon sat fixated, studying the mouse until it scampered away.

Then Simon took a scrap of parchment and began to draw the mouse—not as it had appeared before him, but as it appeared to him in his imagination.

Simon drew and drew until he filled the entire piece of parchment. Then, exhausted, he returned to the dormitory and fell asleep.

The next day, Simon went in search of Father Anselm. This time he did not run, but walked deliberately. He found Father Anselm speaking with Brother William outside the scriptorium.

Simon didn't say a word. He just pulled the parchment from his belt, unrolled it, and handed it to the abbot.

The parchment was covered with Simon's drawings.

As Father Anselm studied them, a smile spread across his face. "Well done, my boy," he said. "Well done, indeed. Now you have understood me fully."

ith one hand, Father Anselm pushed open the door of the scriptorium, and with the other, he beckoned Simon.

"Come, my boy—now that your imagination has awakened, it is time for you to put all of your talents to use in the scriptorium. Not only are there parchments to prepare, pens to cure, pigments to grind, but there are pictures to draw. And not only of mice, but of birds, fish, flowers, trees, insects, people—creatures of all types. For between the pages of each manuscript, there is a world full of wonder to reveal to all those who care to see.

And you, Simon, shall help reveal that world to them!"

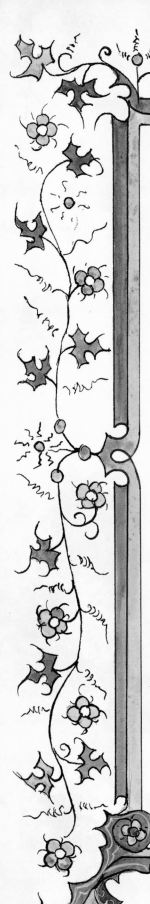

AFTERWORD

The Middle Ages spanned a thousand years, from the fall of the Roman Empire in the fifth century to the beginning of the Renaissance in the fifteenth century. During this time, handmade books called illuminated manuscripts were the most important means people had of recording and preserving their history. Simon lived during this time, around the middle of the eleventh century. It was a time when manuscripts were made by monks living in religious communities called monasteries. Books were important. They told the story of the Church and preserved its history. They also helped to spread the religious beliefs of the Church.

Considering that this was in a time when most people couldn't read, this might seem odd. But it often was the very presence of an illuminated manuscript, with its richly decorated pages, that impressed people, encouraging them to convert to the new faith.

As such, a manuscript was made with great care and with strict concepts in mind, especially when it came to the illustrations, which were not only decorative but also symbolic. That is, each painting told a story: the birth of Jesus, the life of a saint, an episode in the Church's early history. Since most people couldn't read, pictures became an important means of communication.

To communicate these ideas consistently, the monks who completed the decorations, called illuminators, followed established guidelines or conventions. Small details, like the position of a saint's hand, the objects he held, the color of his clothing, were copied exactly, just as the text itself was copied exactly from one manuscript to the next. This made the process of making an illuminated manuscript very tedious.

But illuminators are artists, and artists like to have a free hand in what they create. So where in all of this was the illuminator given the freedom to exercise his artistic creativity? If the text was copied exactly from an existing book and the decorative patterns and major images followed strict design conventions, where could an illuminator let his imagination run wild?

There were several places. In an inventive text correction, often done humorously between two lines of text or sometimes, when a large block of text was overlooked, in the margins. In an attractive line filler that extended a short line of text to the margin using decorative patterns. In the margins, the open space that surrounded the central text and images.

It was in the margins that an illuminator unleashed his imagination. It was in the margins where individual creativity ran wild. It was in the margins that Simon found the answer to Father Anselm's puzzle.

DATE DUE		